· A CHINESE LEGEND ·
Once There Were No Pandas

by MARGARET GREAVES

illustrated by BEVERLEY GOODING

E. P. DUTTON   NEW YORK

First published in England 1985 by Methuen Children's Books Ltd,
11 New Fetter Lane, London EC4P 4EE

Published in the United States 1985 by E. P. Dutton,
2 Park Avenue, New York, N.Y. 10016

Text copyright © 1985 by Margaret Greaves
based on a Chinese legend remembered by Michael de Havilland

Illustrations copyright © 1985 by Beverley Gooding

Library of Congress Cataloging in Publication Data

Greaves, Margaret.
    Once there were no pandas.

    "Based on a Chinese legend remembered by Michael
de Havilland"—
    Summary: In the forests of China in ancient times,
a small girl's sacrifice for a friendly white bear
brings about the appearance of the first pandas.
    [1. Folklore—China. 2. Pandas—Fiction] I. Gooding,
Beverley, ill.   II. De Havilland, Michael.   III. Title.
PZ8.1.G755On 1985   398.2'45297443'0951 [E] 85-7033
ISBN 0-525-44211-1

Printed in Great Britain   OBE   First Edition
10 9 8 7 6 5 4 3 2 1

Chinese Characters and Pronunciation

Chien-min: pronounced Chee' en-min
the name of the little girl

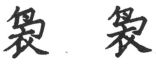

Niao Niao: pronounced Nee'ow Nee'ow
the name of the little bear; it also means "very soft"

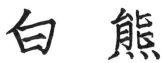

bai xiong: pronounced bye see'ong
white bear

xiong mao: pronounced see'ong mao
pandas

Guan-yin: pronounced Guan-yin
Goddess of Mercy

Long, long ago in China, when the earth and stars were young, there were none of the black-and-white bears that the Chinese call *xiong mao* and that we call pandas. But deep in the bamboo forests lived bears with fur as white and soft and shining as new-fallen snow. The Chinese called them *bai xiong*, which means "white bear."

In a small house at the edge of the forest lived a peasant and his wife and their little daughter, Chien-min. *chee 'en-min*

One very hot day, Chien-min was playing alone at the edge of the forest. The green shadow of the trees looked cool as water, and a patch of yellow buttercups shone invitingly.

"They are only *just* inside the forest," said the little girl to herself. "It will take only a minute to pick some."

She slipped in among the trees. But when she had picked her flowers, she looked around, puzzled. There were so many small paths! Which one led back to the village?

As she hesitated, something moved and rustled among
the leaves nearby. She saw a delicate head with big ears,
a slim body dappled with light and shadow. It was one of
the small deer of the forest. Chien-min had startled it, and
it bounded away between the trees. She tried to follow,
hoping it might lead her home. But almost at once it was
out of sight, and Chien-min was completely lost.

She began to be frightened. But then she heard another sound—something whimpering not far away. She ran toward the place, forgetting her fear, wanting only to help.

There, close to a big thorny bush, squatted a very small white bear cub. Every now and then he shook one of his front paws and licked it, then whimpered again.

"Oh, you poor little one!" Chien-min ran over and knelt beside the little bear. "Don't cry! I'll help you. Let me see it."

The cub seemed to understand. He let her take hold
of his paw. Between the pads was a very sharp thorn.
Chien-min pinched it between her finger and thumb,
and very carefully drew it out. The cub rubbed his
head against her hands as she stroked him.

A moment later, a huge white bear came crashing through the trees, growling fiercely. But when she saw that the little girl was only playing with her cub, her anger vanished. She licked his paw, then nuzzled Chien-min as if she too were one of her cubs.

The mother bear was so gentle that the child took courage and put her arms round her neck, stroking the soft fur. "How beautiful you are!" she said. "Oh, if only you could show me the way home."

At once the great bear ambled forward, grunting to the cub and his new friend to follow. Fearlessly now, Chien-min held on to the thick white coat and very soon found that she was at the edge of the forest again, close to her own home.

From that day on, she often went into the forest. Her parents were happy about it, knowing their daughter was safe under the protection of the great white bear. She met many of the other bears too, and many of their young, but her special friend was always the little cub she had helped. She called him Niao Niao, which means "very soft," because his fur was so fine and beautiful.

The mother bear showed the little girl her secret home,
a den in the hollow of a great tree. Chien-min went there
many times, played with the cubs, and learned the ways
of the forest. Always the great she-bear led her safely
back before nightfall.

One warm spring afternoon, Chien-min was sitting by the hollow tree, watching the cubs at play, when she saw a stealthy movement between the bamboos. A wide, whiskered face. Fierce topaz eyes. Small tufted ears. A glimpse of spotted, silky fur.

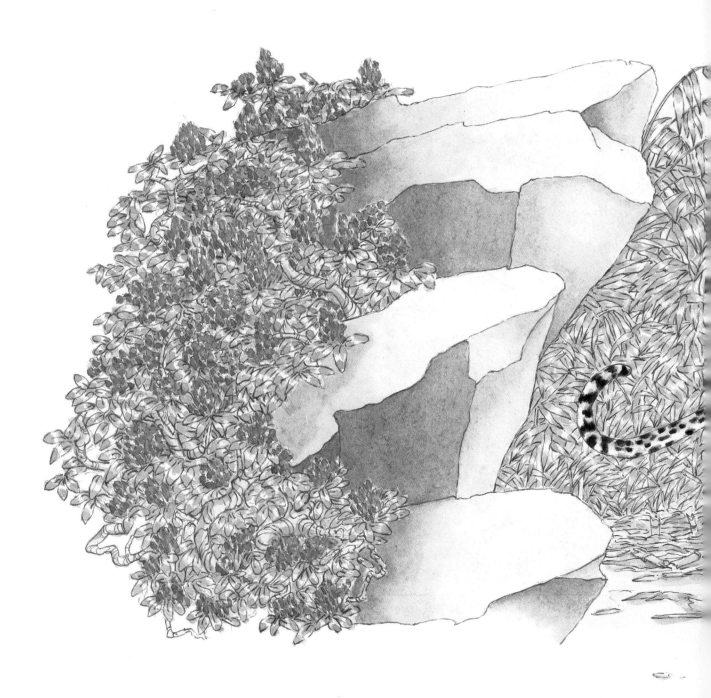

Chien-min sprang up, shouting a warning. But she was too late. With bared teeth and lashing tail, the hungry leopard had leaped upon Niao Niao.

Chien-min forgot all fear in her love for her friend.
Snatching up a great stone, she hurled it at the leopard.
The savage beast dropped his prey but turned on her,
snarling with fury. At the same moment, the she-bear
charged through the trees like a thunderbolt.

The leopard backed off, terrified by her anger. But as
he turned to run, he struck out at Chien-min with his huge
claws, knocking her to the ground.

The bears ran to Chien-min, growling and whining and licking her face. But the little girl never moved. She had saved Niao Niao's life by the loss of her own.

News of her death swept through the forest. From
miles away, north, south, east and west, all the white bears
gathered to mourn. They wept and whimpered for their
lost friend, rubbing their paws in the dust of the earth and

wiping the tears from their eyes. As they did so, the wet dust left great black smears across their faces. They beat their paws against their bodies in bitter lamentation, and the wet dust clung to their fur in wide black bands.

But although the bears sorrowed for Chien-min, and her parents and friends mourned her, they were all comforted to know that she was happy. Guan-yin, the beautiful Goddess of Mercy, would give her a special place in heaven, where her selfless love for her friend would always be rewarded.

And from that day to this, there have been no white bears, *bai xiong*, anywhere in China. Instead there are the great black-and-white bears, *xiong mao*, that we call pandas, still mourning for their lost friend, Chien-min.